ELEPHANT WALK

GW00793044

CONTENTS

ALL ABOUT ELEPHANTS

Elephants are **mammals**. They are the biggest land animals. There are two kinds of elephants: **African elephants** and **Asian elephants**.

African elephants are bigger than Asian elephants. They also have bigger ears. Most African elephants have tusks. However, many Asian elephants don't have tusks at all.

African elephant

Asian elephant

3

All elephants have thick,
wrinkled skin. They have
big ears and long trunks.

Elephants use their trunks
to get food and water.
Elephant trunks are very heavy.
Sometimes elephants rest them
over their tusks.

Elephants are clever animals.
They can communicate with
each other over long distances.
They have an excellent sense
of smell and hearing.
They can hear sounds
that humans cannot hear.

ELEPHANT FAMILIES

Elephants live in small groups called **herds**. There are usually 10 to 20 elephants in a herd.

The leader of the herd is an old female elephant called the **matriarch**.

Elephant herds are made up of female elephants and their young. All of the elephants in the herd help look after the younger elephants.

When young male elephants
are about 12 years old,
they move to a **bachelor herd**
of male elephants.

Older **bull elephants** often
live on their own, joining
the main herd only during
the mating season.

A baby elephant can walk
very soon after it is born.
It drinks milk from its mother.

Other females in the herd
are called aunts. They help
look after the baby elephant
and protect it from **predators**.

Elephants are friendly animals.
When elephants meet,
they put their trunks together
as if to say "hello".

Elephants are loyal to their
families. They stay with the herd
for life. When one of the herd
dies, the others are very sad.

When an elephant is sick, the other elephants help it walk to food and water.

If an elephant falls down, the others will help it up and let it lean on them.

WALKING TO WATER

Elephants walk from place
to place in search of food
and water. During dry times,
the matriarch seems to know
where water can be found.

Elephants like to bathe in water.
They also like to spray
themselves with dust, or roll
in mud. The dust and mud
protect them from insect bites
and sunburn.

WHAT'S FOR DINNER?

Elephants are **herbivores**.
They pick grass and leaves with their trunks. They use their trunks to tear down branches and trees. Elephants can also strip the bark off trees with their tusks.

ELEPHANTS AND PEOPLE

In Asia, people and elephants have worked together for nearly 5,000 years. Beautifully painted and decorated, elephants also take part in festivals in some countries around the world.

In parts of Africa and Asia, areas have been set aside for elephants to roam freely. People can visit these parks to see elephants in their natural home.

GLOSSARY

African elephant – an elephant that comes only from parts of Africa

Asian elephant – an elephant that comes only from parts of India and Southeast Asia

bachelor herd – a group of young male elephants that live together

bull elephant – an older male elephant

herbivore – an animal that eats only plants

herd – a group of elephants

mammal – an animal that feeds its young milk

matriarch – an old female elephant that leads the herd

predator – an animal that eats other animals